WHY DO WE SING?

For Elaia

Why Do We Sing?
Text copyright © 2024 by Sam Tsui & Casey Breves
Illustrations copyright © 2024 by Sam Tsui

Library of Congress Control Number: 2023942528
ISBN 978-0-06-330594-6

The artist used Adobe Photoshop to create the digital illustrations for this book.
Book design by Marisa Rother
24 25 26 27 28 RTLO 10 9 8 7 6 5 4 3 2 1
First Edition

WHY DO WE SING?

Written by **SAM TSUI** & **CASEY BREVES**
Illustrated by **SAM TSUI**

HARPER
An Imprint of HarperCollinsPublishers

Why do we sing?
Hum a tune?
Belt out a melody?

Why do we make music with our voices?
Well, let's see · · ·

We sing because we're happy

or to say, "I feel strong."

When we sing together
we know that we **belong**.

A song can help us fall asleep

or say, "I love you!"

Shepherds sing to call their sheep—

"Yo-del-o-del-ay-hee-hoo!"

Some sing to **entertain** a crowd,

with friends or on their own.

Songs help us **remember** how to find our way back home.

Anthems, shanties, chants,

duets, carols sung by choirs,

melodies both old and new

can be shared
around the fire.

We sing at parties   or in prayer—

Some songs are just for fun;

some speak **truth** to power.

Every song's important
and I hope now it's clear

why we all love to sing so much!
I just can't wait to hear . . .

What will **YOU** sing?